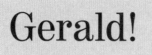

First, you said,
"It's *book* time."

Then, you said,
"It's *shoe* time."

Which time is it?

It's SHOE TIME!

MO WILLEMS' ELEPHANT & PIGGIE LIKE READING!

By Bryan Collier
CORETTA SCOTT KING AWARD WINNER AND CALDECOTT HONOR RECIPIENT

An **ELEPHANT & PIGGIE LIKE READING!** Book

Hyperion Books for Children / *New York*

AN IMPRINT OF DISNEY BOOK GROUP

To every kid who dares to be different
—B.C.

PAT!

PAT!

PAT!

PAT!

Elephant & Piggie Like Reading! is an early reader series created and coedited by Mo Willems. The series features exciting new stories from renowned award-winning authors and illustrators.

First Edition, November 2017
1 3 5 7 9 10 8 6 4 2
FAC-034274-17265
Printed in the United States of America

This book is set in Century 725/Monotype; Grilled Cheese BTN/Fontbros; Neutraface, Fink, Typography of Coop/House Industries
Designed by Tyler Nevins

Library of Congress Cataloging-in-Publication Data

Names: Willems, Mo, author, illustrator. Collier, Bryan, author, illustrator.
Title: It's shoe time! / by [Mo Willems and] Bryan Collier. Other titles: It is shoe time!
Description: First edition. New York : Hyperion Books for Children, an imprint of Disney Book Group, [2017]
Series: Elephant & Piggie like reading! Summary: If you choose to wear unmatched shoes, can they still be a pair?
Identifiers: LCCN 2017018076 ISBN 9781484726471 (hardback)
Subjects: CYAC: Shoes—Fiction. Humorous stories. BISAC: JUVENILE
    FICTION / Concepts / General. JUVENILE FICTION / Humorous Stories.
    JUVENILE FICTION / Social Issues / Values & Virtues.
Classification: LCC PZ7.W65535 It 2017   DDC [E]—dc23
LC record available at https://lccn.loc.gov/2017018076

Reinforced binding
Visit hyperionbooksforchildren.com and pigeonpresents.com

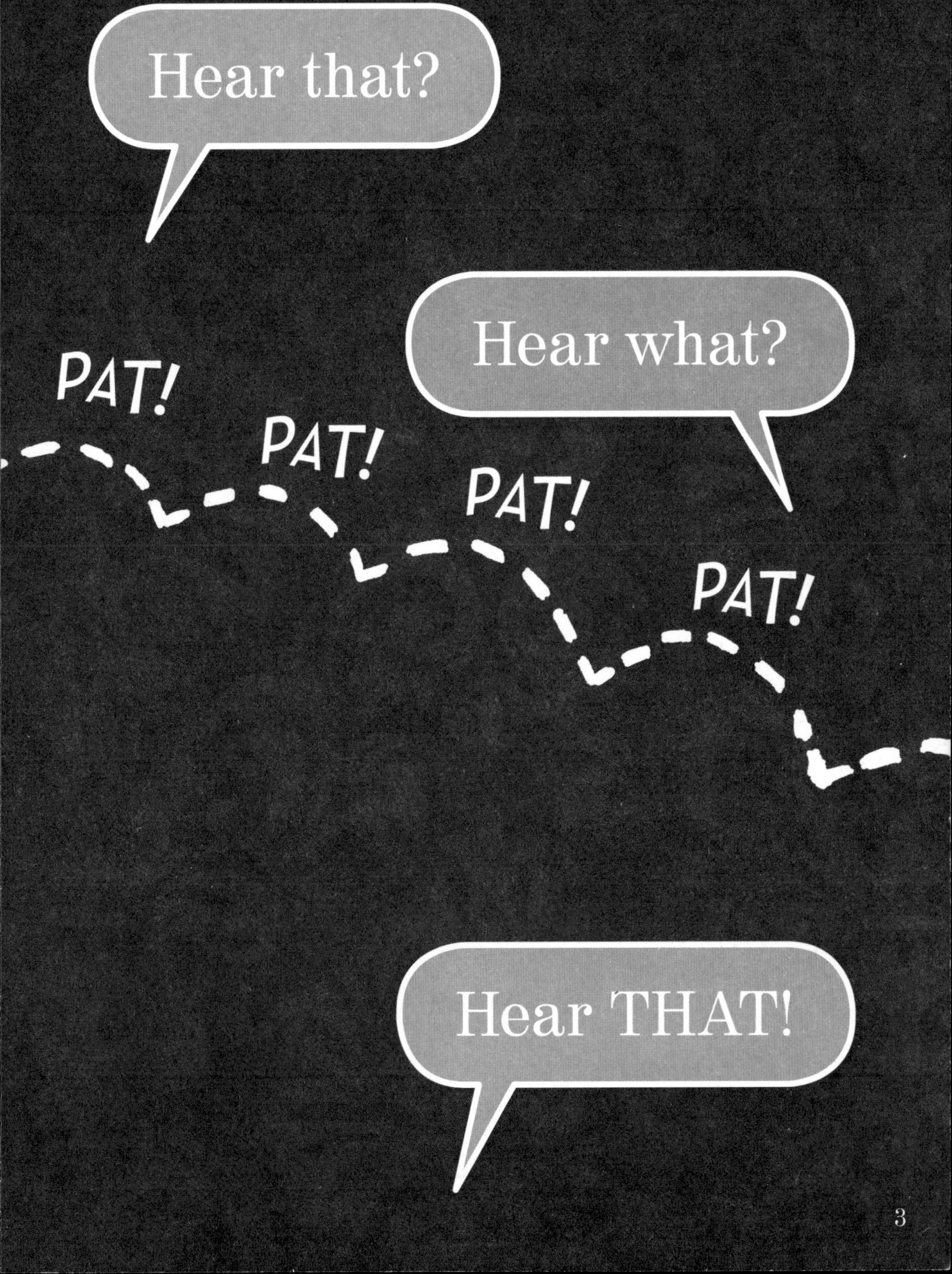
Hear that?
PAT!
PAT!
Hear what?
PAT!
PAT!
Hear THAT!

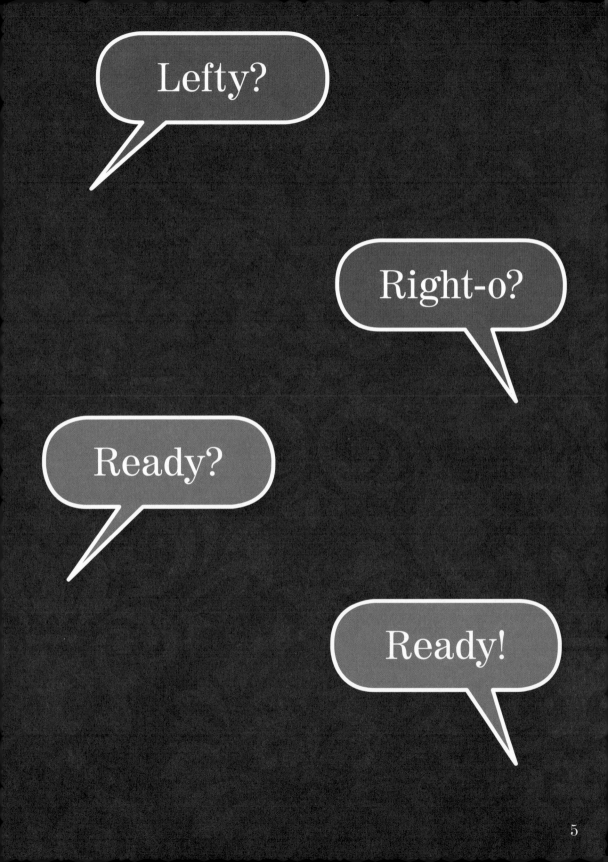

Will I choose *Flip-Flops*?
Yes! Yes! Yessssss!
FLIP!
FLOP!
Or maybe . . . No, no, noooooo!

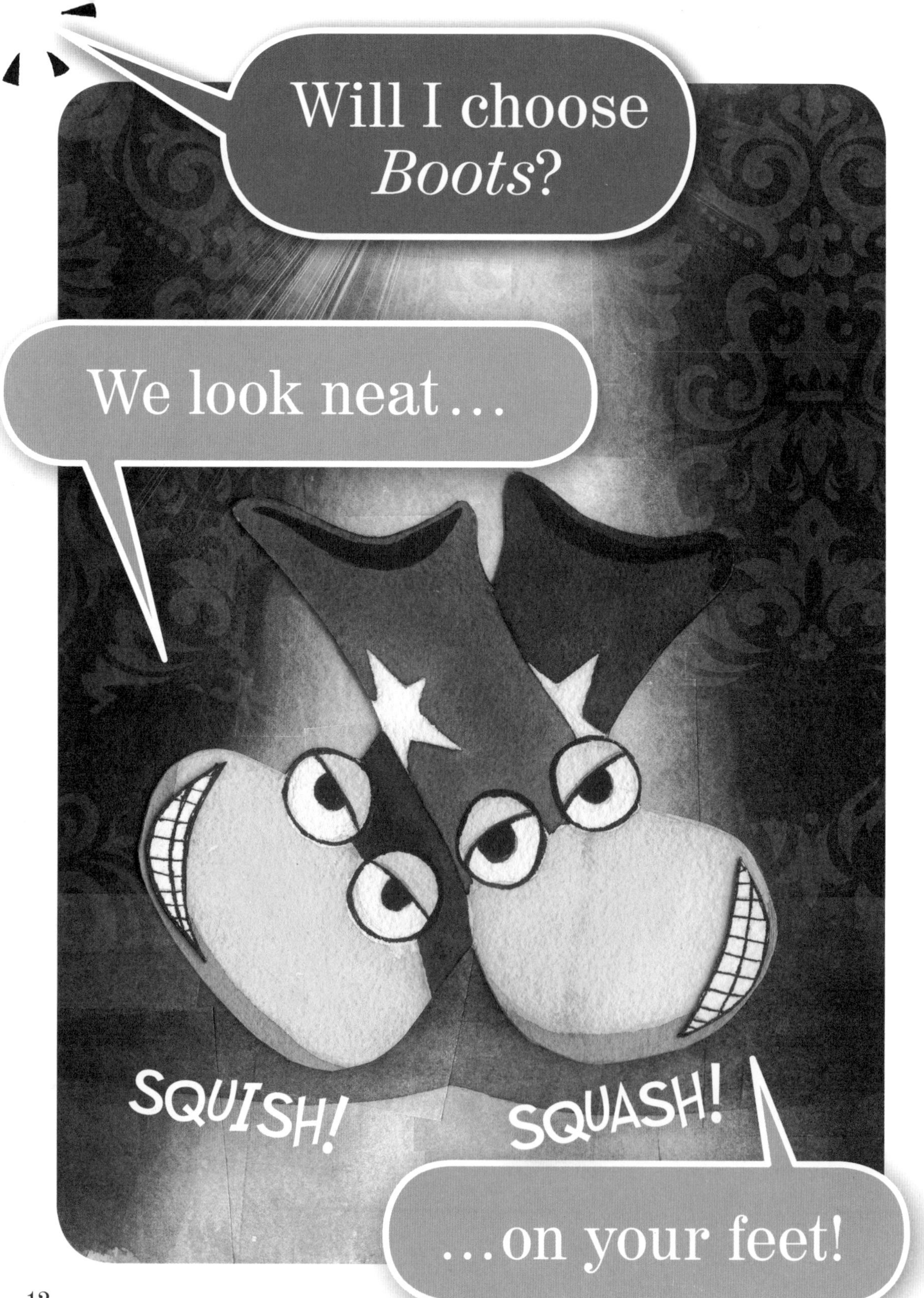
Will I choose *Boots*?
We look neat…
SQUISH!
SQUASH!
…on your feet!

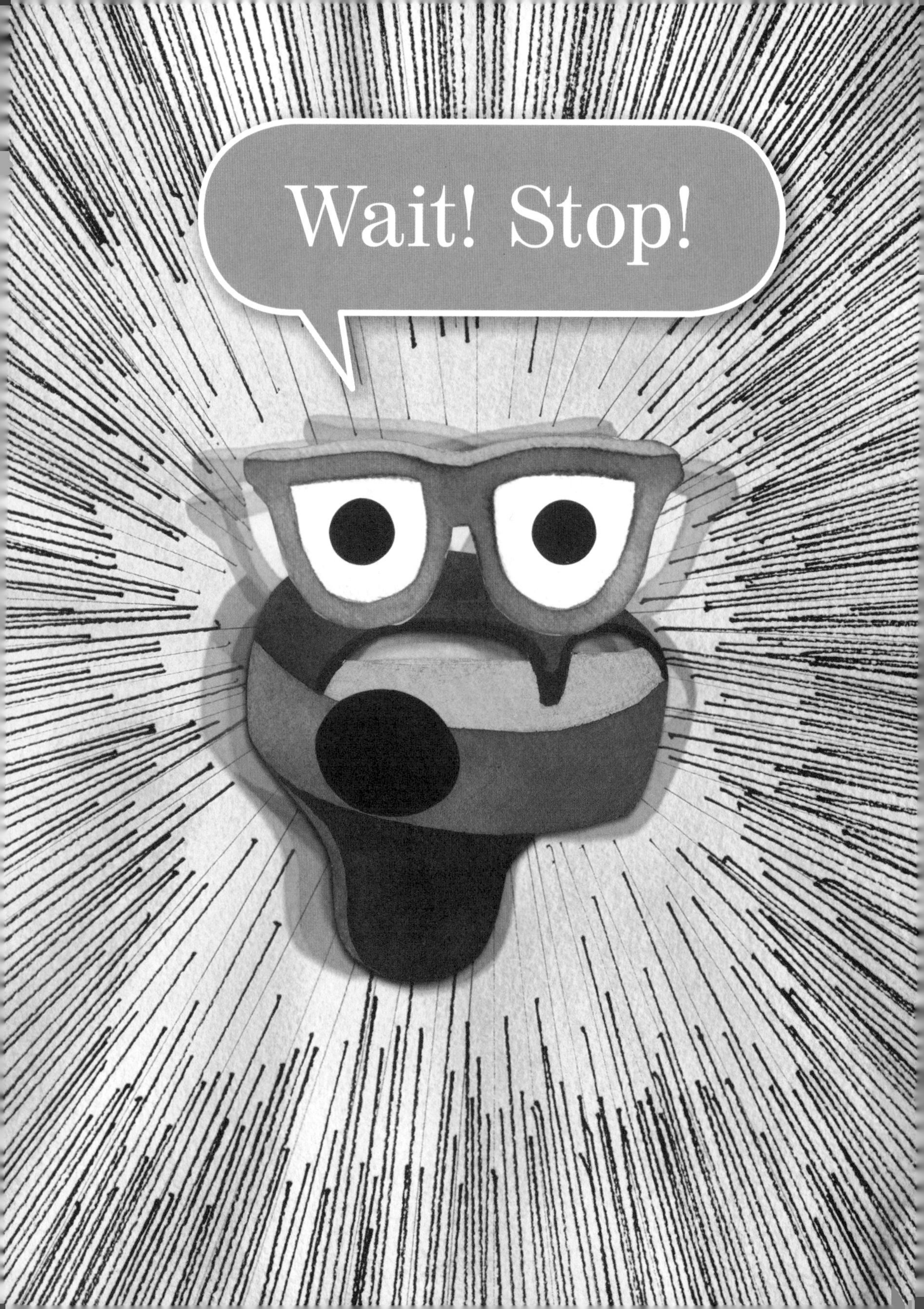
Wait! Stop!

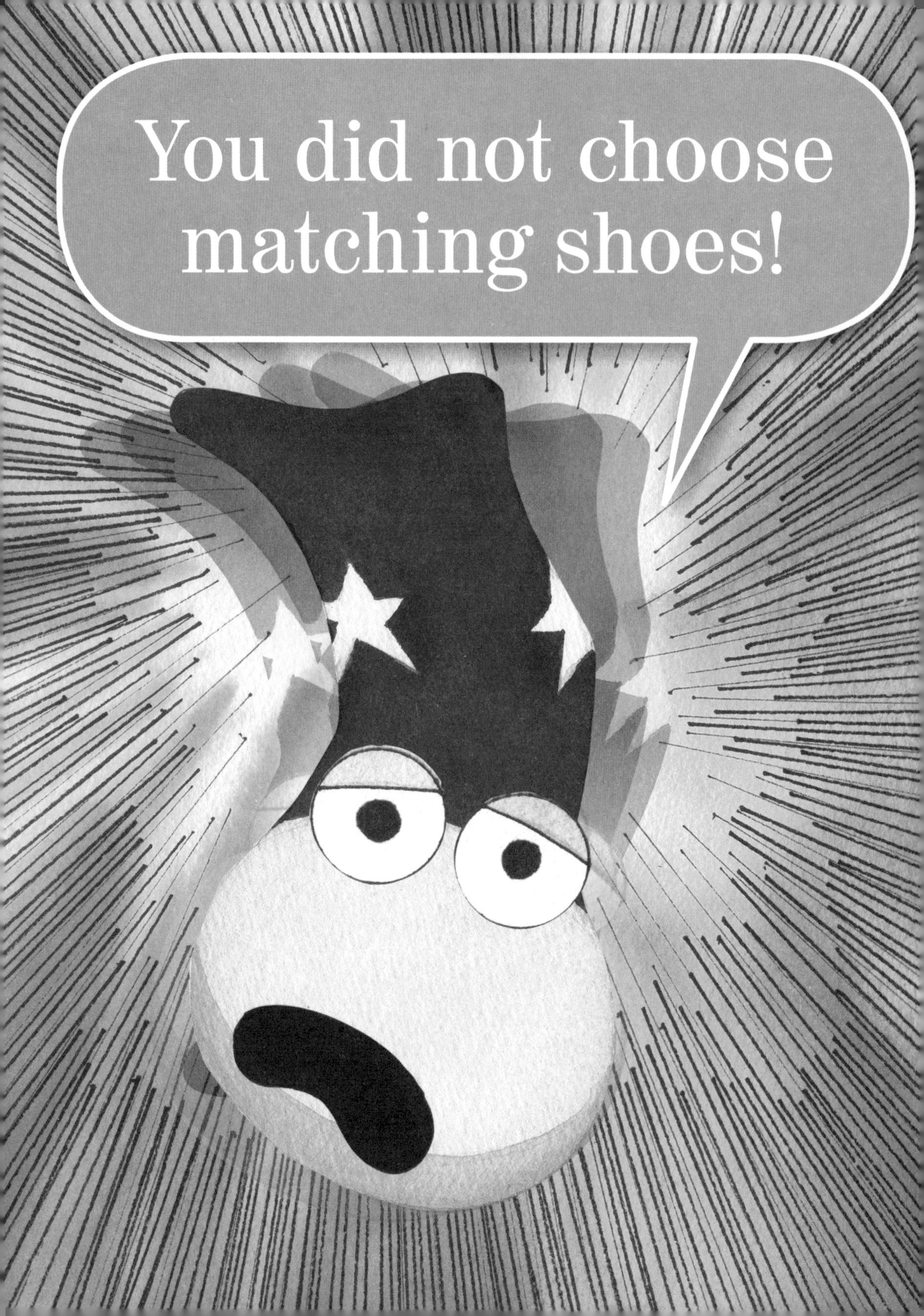
You did not choose matching shoes!

20

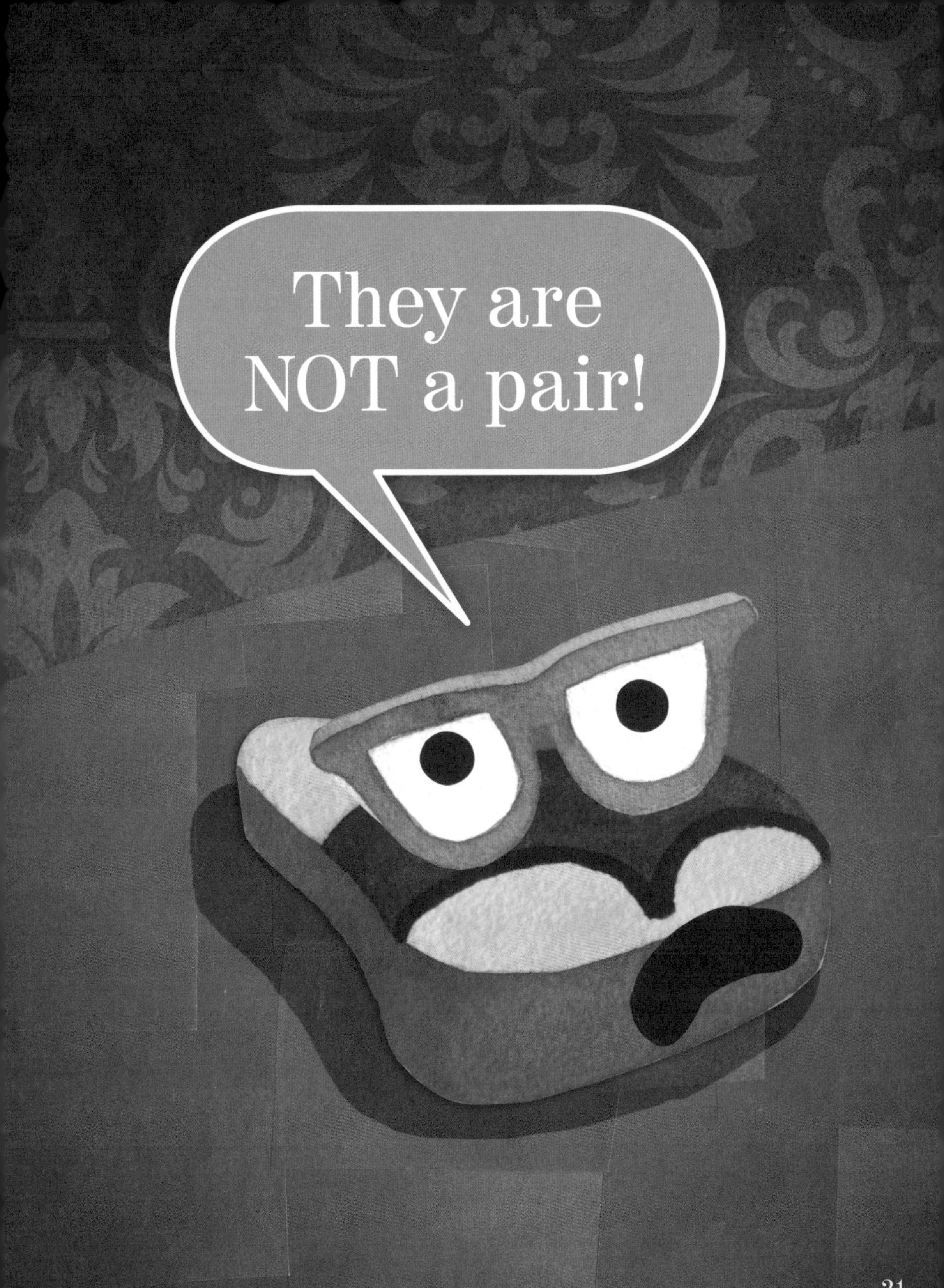
They are NOT a pair!

23

26

27

29

That way!

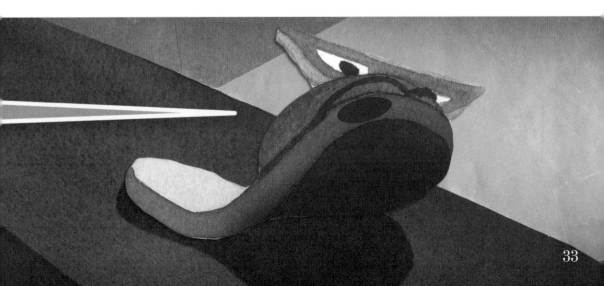

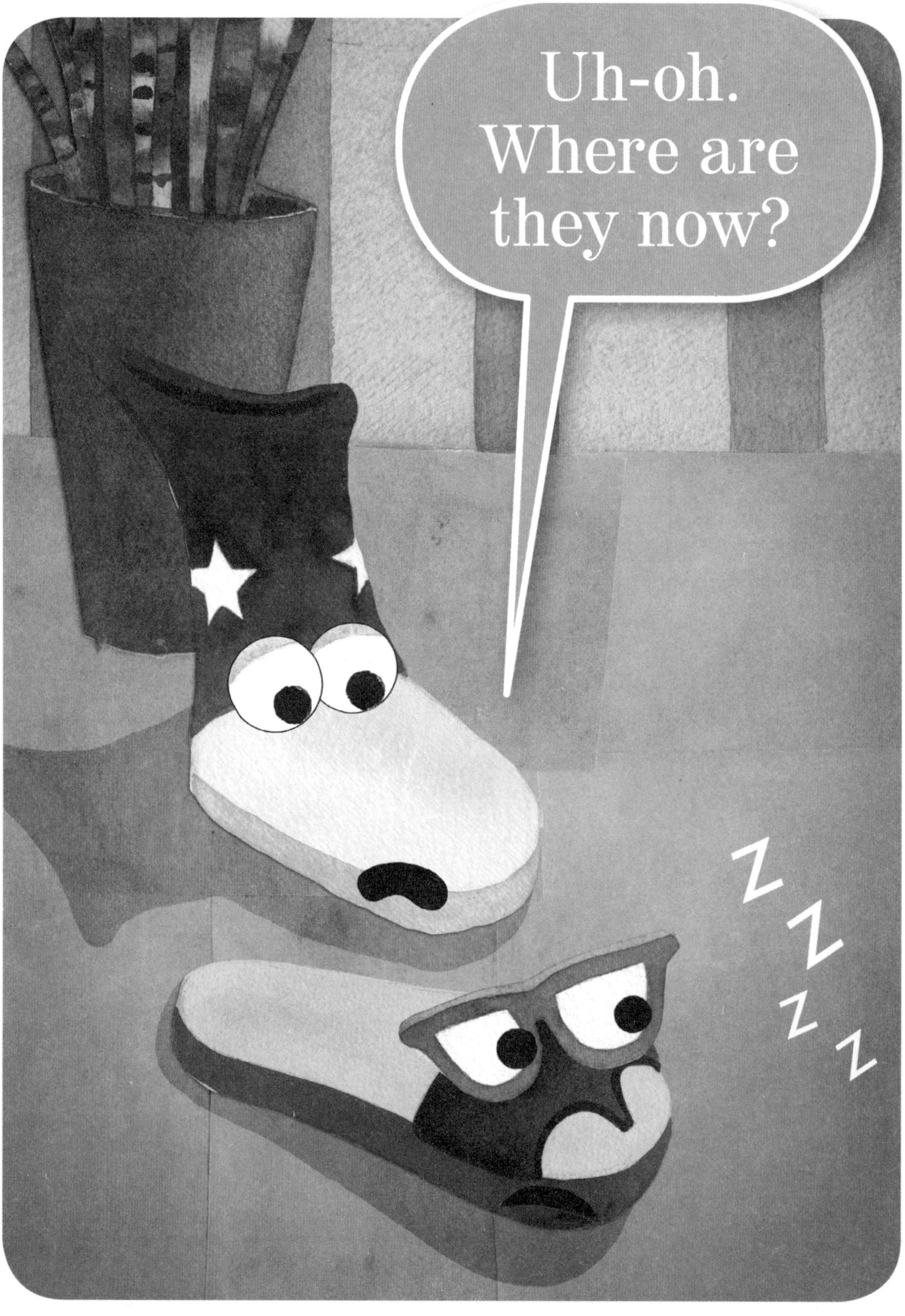
Uh-oh. Where are they now?
Z Z Z Z Z

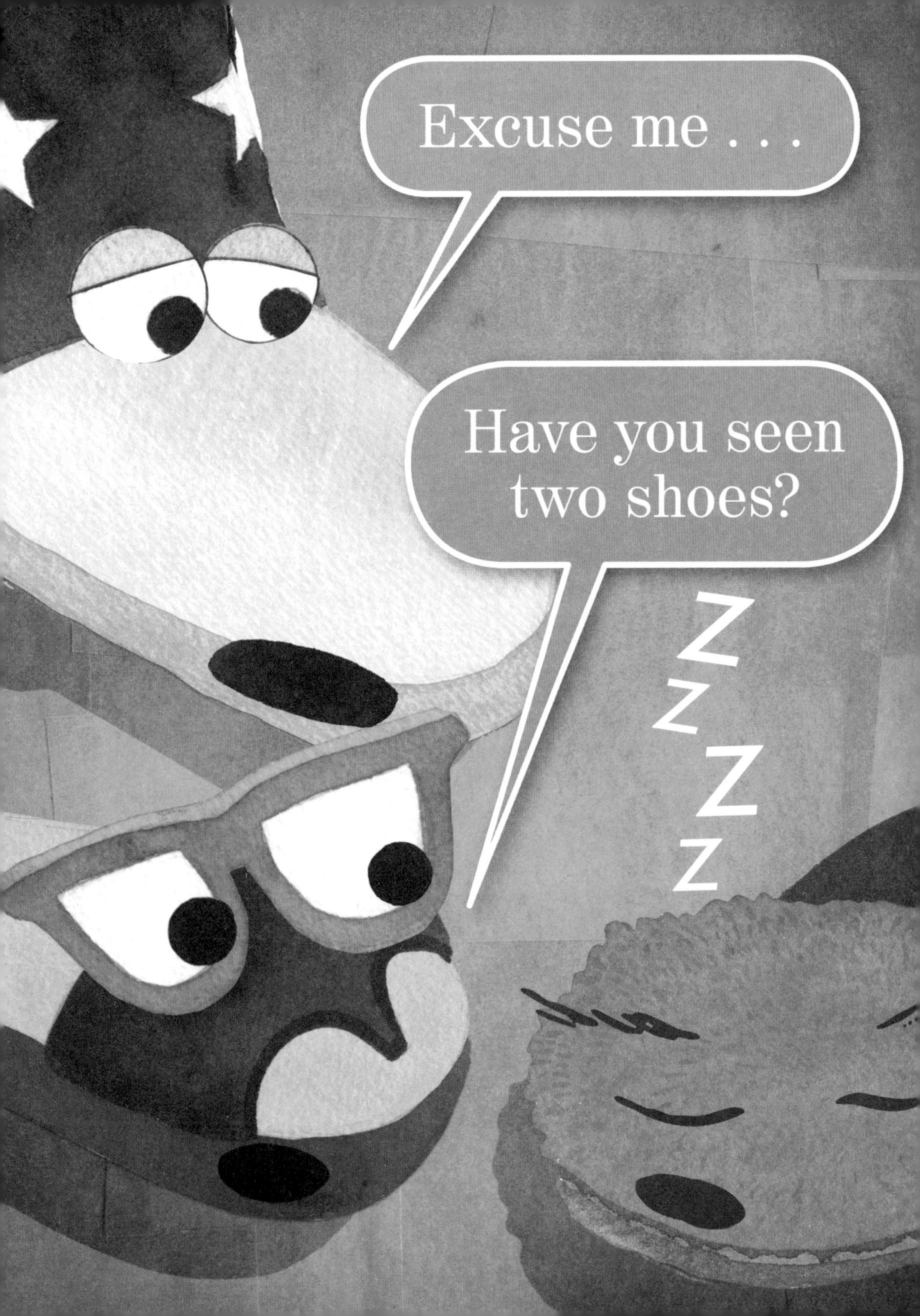
Excuse me . . .
Have you seen two shoes?
ZZZZ

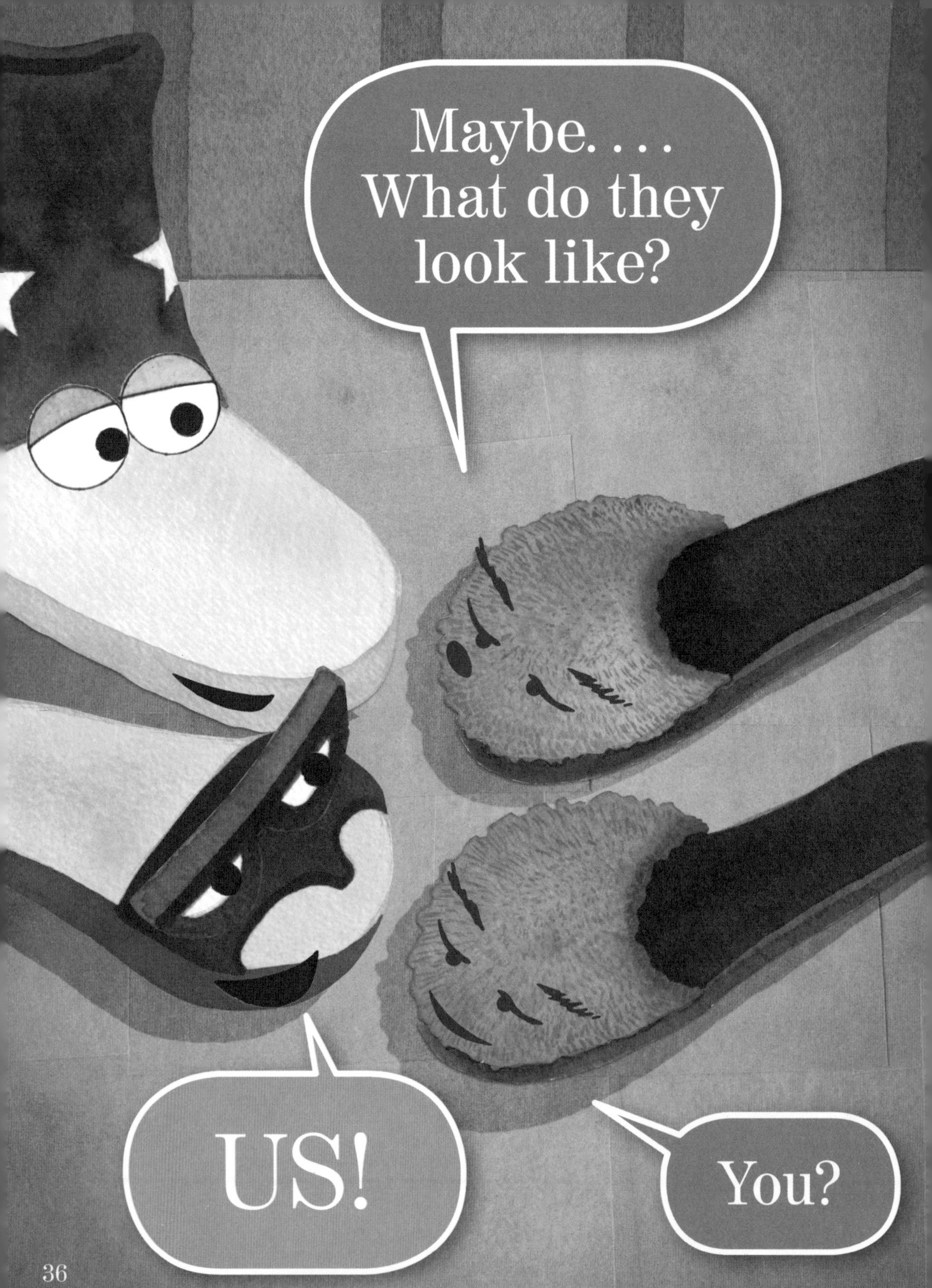
Maybe. . . .
What do they
look like?
US!
You?

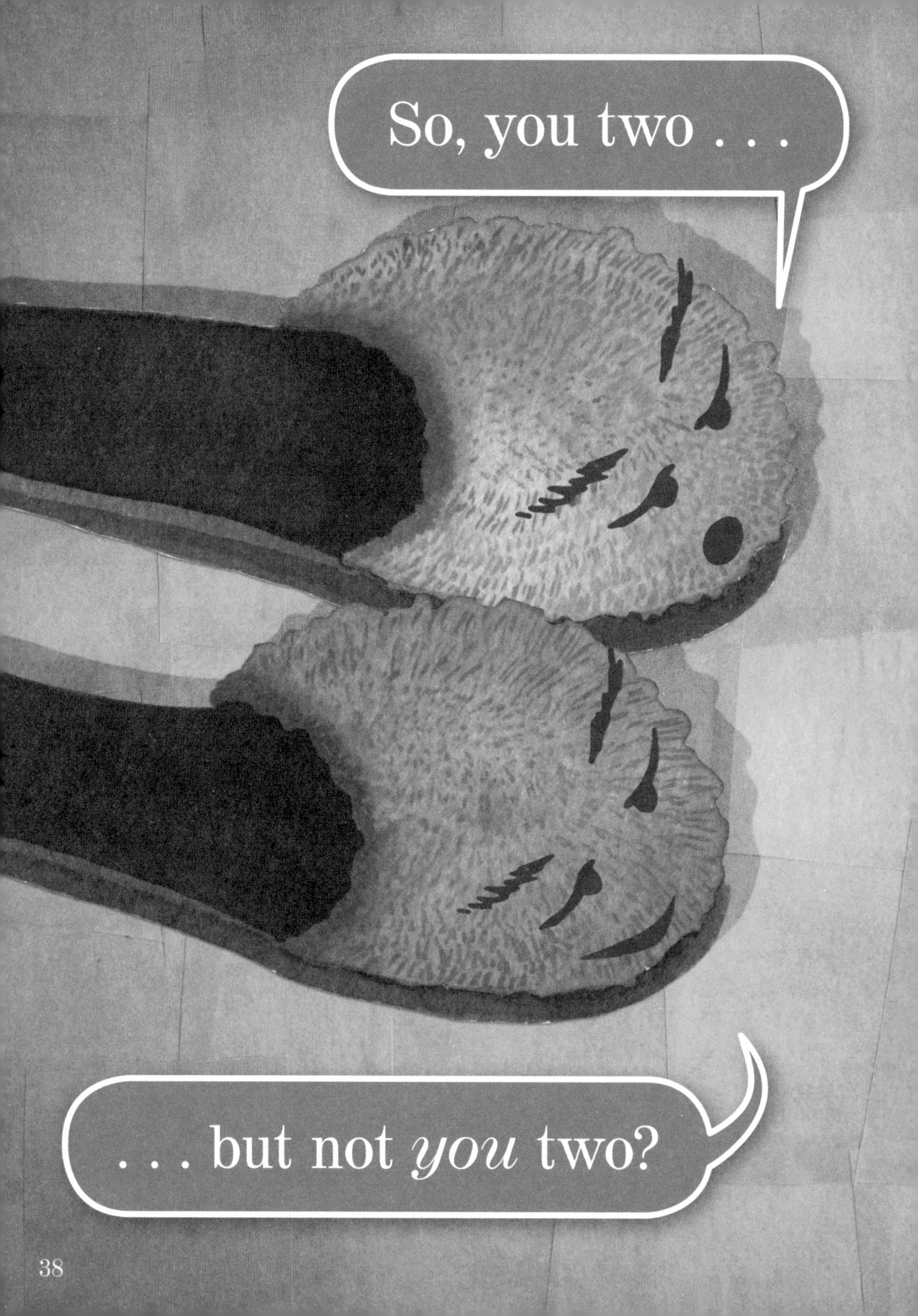
So, you two . . .
. . . but not *you* two?

39

41

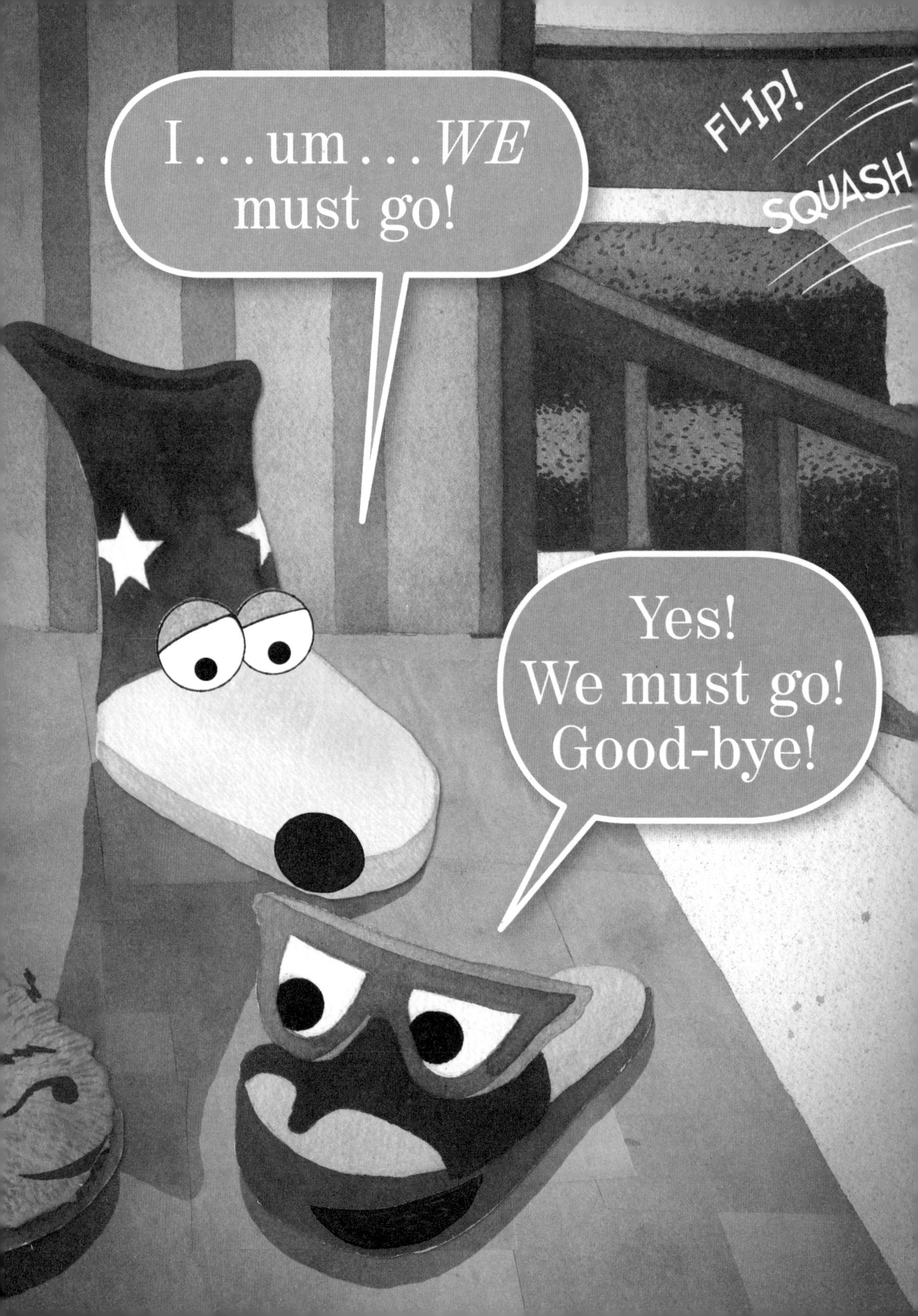
I . . . um . . . *WE* must go!
FLIP!
SQUASH
Yes! We must go! Good-bye!

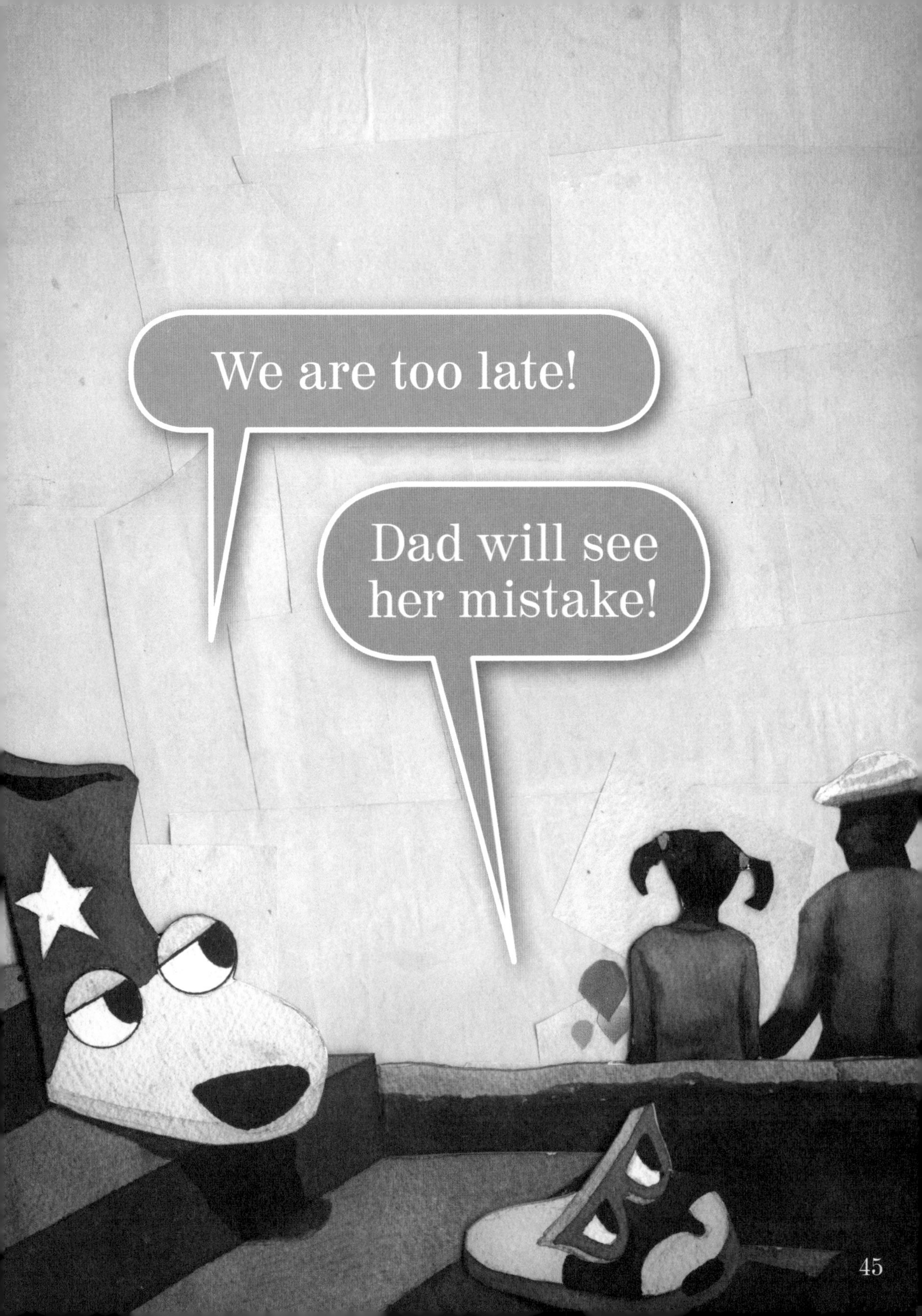

We are too late!
Dad will see her mistake!

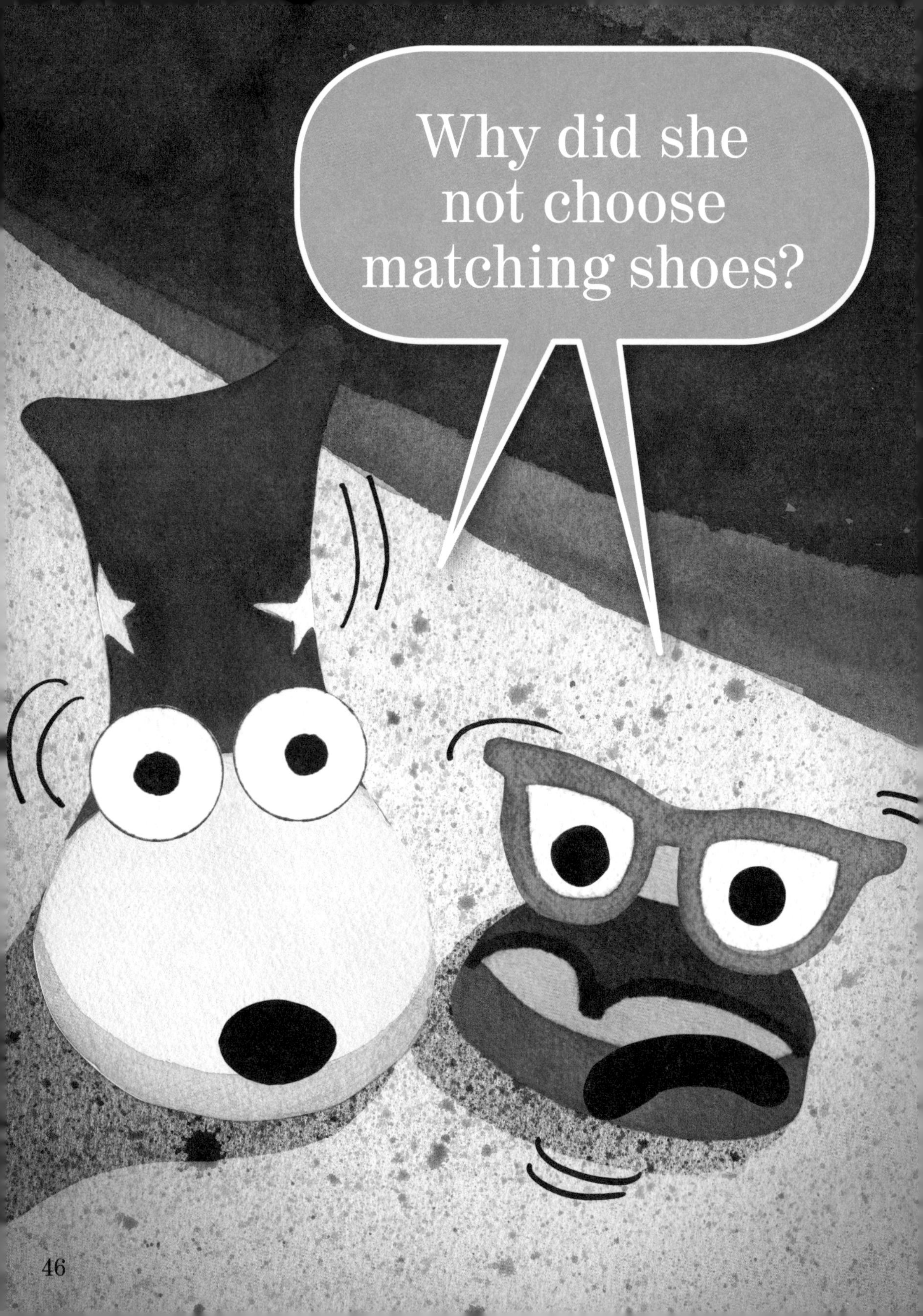
Why did she not choose matching shoes?

47

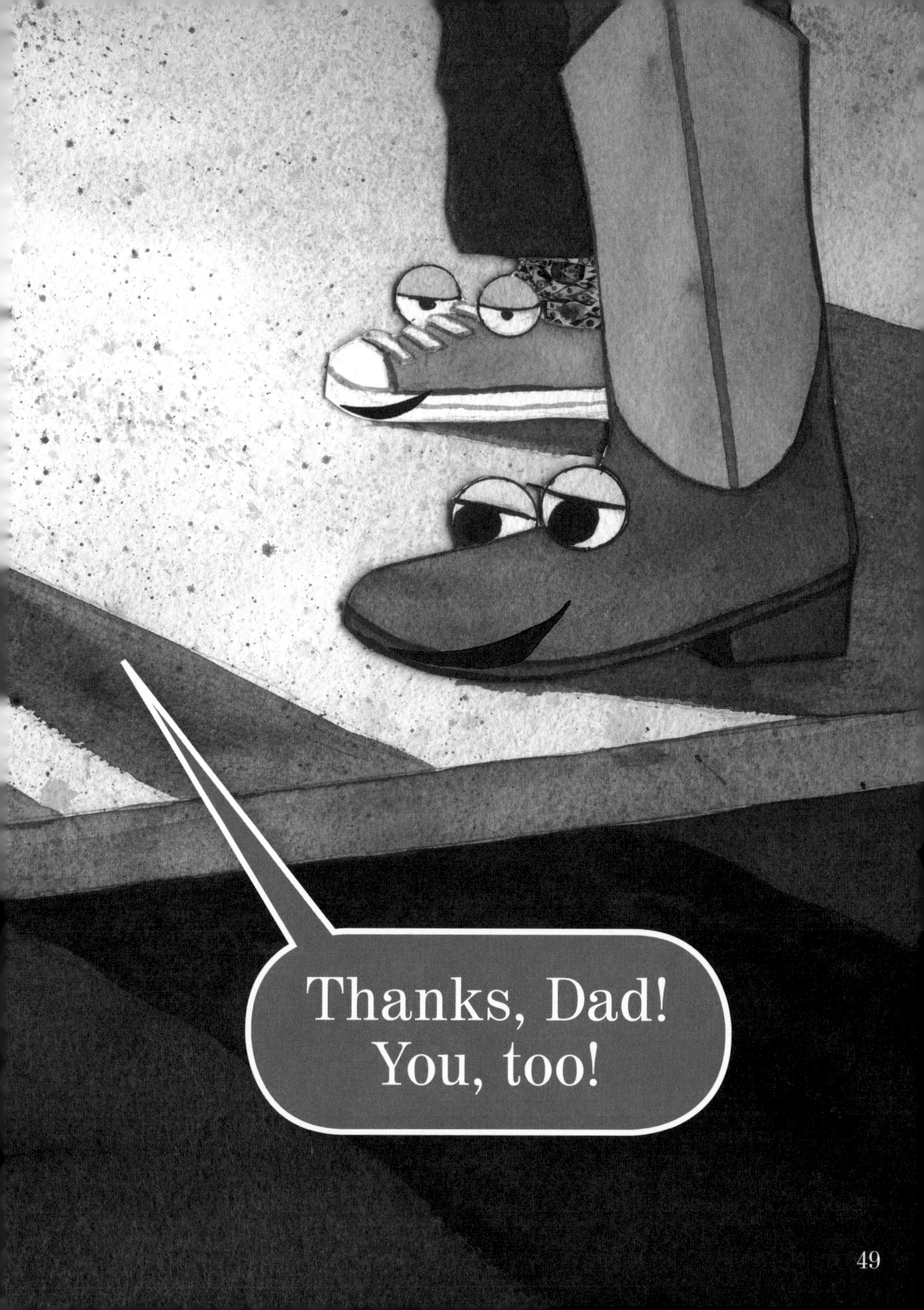
Thanks, Dad!
You, too!

**Elephant & Piggie
also like reading:**

The Cookie Fiasco
by Dan Santat

We Are Growing!
by Laurie Keller
(Theodor Seuss Geisel Medal)

The Good for Nothing Button!
by Charise Mericle Harper